This Ladybird ......gs to

Brianna Tunks

Stories and rhymes in this book

Happy Birthday, Leo!

Being four is great!

Leo's wobbly tooth

Leo's list

Moochy mud
 and hidey-holes

I'm me!

Well done, Leo

I'm coming after you!

All Ladybird books are available at most bookshops,
supermarkets and newsagents, or can be ordered direct from:
Ladybird Postal Sales
PO Box 133 Paignton TQ3 2YP England
Telephone: (+44) 01803 554761
Fax: (+44) 01803 663394

A catalogue record for this book is available
from the British Library

Published by Ladybird Books Ltd
A subsidiary of the Penguin Group
A Pearson Company
© LADYBIRD BOOKS LTD MCMXCVIII

LADYBIRD and the device of a Ladybird are trademarks of
Ladybird Books Ltd Loughborough Leicestershire UK

Lion Stories
for 4 year olds

by Geraldine Taylor
illustrated by Rebecca Archer

Happy Birthday, Leo!

Leo gave the loudest *ROAR* ever.

"It's my *BIRTHDAY* today! And I'm going to win *ALL* the prizes at my party!"

"What about your friends?" said Mum.

"But it's *MY* birthday," said Leo.

At five o'clock, Leo's friends arrived for his party.

At the party feast, Leo was very good. He didn't grab all his favourite chocolate biscuits. And he even helped Baby Leopard take a huge piece of birthday cake.

Then it was time for the games.
Leo wanted to win *ALL* the prizes.

The first game was Stick The Tail
On Zebra. Elephant closed his eyes,
and stuck the tail… on Zebra's back!

Then Giraffe closed his eyes, and
stuck the tail… on Zebra's ear!

Baby Leopard closed his eyes, and
stuck the tail… on Zebra's foot!

At last it was Leo's turn. He closed his eyes, and stuck the tail... on Zebra's nose! Everyone burst out laughing.

"I think we'll give this prize to Zebra for being so patient," said Mum.

"Grrmph," thought Leo. "But it's *MY* birthday." He felt like sulking.

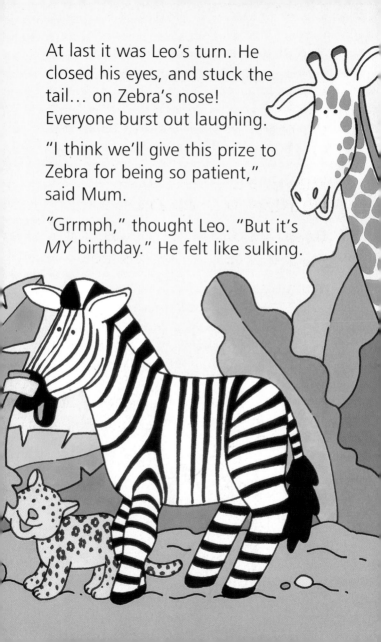

The next game was Hide and Squeak.
Everyone hid and Mum had to find
the one with the loudest squeak.

"I'm sure to win," thought Leo…

Elephant's squeak sounded like
a grumbly burp.

Giraffe's squeak sounded like
a wheezy whistle.

Zebra's squeak sounded like
a snorty snuffle.

As for Leo, his squeak sounded like a growly bark. Baby Leopard was the only one who could squeak properly.

"Baby Leopard wins the prize," said Mum.

"Grrmph," thought Leo. "It's *MY* birthday." And he was just about to sulk when Mum called, "Musical Beanbags!"

"I'll win *this* game," thought Leo.

Mum laid out four beanbags and put on some music.

Round and round they went, and then the music stopped… Baby Leopard was out.

Round and round they went, and then the music stopped… Giraffe was out.

Round and round they went, and then the music stopped… Zebra was out.

"I'm sure to win now," thought Leo.

Round and round they went, then the music stopped… and Elephant planted his big fat bottom on the last beanbag. Poor Leo was out!

"That's the end of the games," said Mum. "It's time for everyone to go home…" But she saw that Leo was looking sad.

"Well, one more game then," she said. "For the very last prize, let's play Sleeping Lions."

"Oh, NO!" thought Leo. "I don't like this game. I can *NEVER* keep still."

So everyone lay down and tried to keep very, very still. Mum tiptoed all round them, looking and listening.

It was very, very *HARD* pretending to be a sleeping lion.

Baby Leopard tried… but wriggled.

Elephant tried… but wobbled.

Giraffe tried… but giggled.

"You're *ALL* out," whispered Mum. "All except…"

Everyone looked at Leo. He was fast asleep.

"Wake up, Leo!" laughed Mum. "It's *your* turn to win the prize." And Mum gave a sleepy Leo his very special prize – a glittery golden crown.

"This is the best birthday I've *EVER HAD*," roared Leo.

Being four is great!

I'm four years old and all grown up.
It's been a long time to wait.
*I'm a lion who's four, and I can **ROAR**.*
Being four is really great!

I can ride my bike and write my name
And reach the highest shelf.
I can brush my teeth and comb my mane,
And get dressed by myself!

Leo's

wobbly tooth

"My front tooth's all wobbly," said Leo.

"Let's see…" said Hippo. "OOOOH, look – it is all wobbly, it *really* is!"

"Can I have a wobble?" said Zebra.

"My turn!" said Elephant. "Wobble it for me, Leo."

All the other animals queued up to see Leo wobble his tooth.

Leo felt really proud. No one else had a tooth that wobbled!

But at lunchtime, something awful happened. Crocodile came to see Leo's wobbly tooth, but when Leo opened his mouth – the tooth had gone.

"Where's my wobbly tooth?" roared Leo.

Everyone searched and searched...
but Leo's tooth was nowhere to
be found.

"What if I've swallowed it?"
gasped Leo.

Just then, Mum appeared.

"Look what I've found behind the big rock," she said.

"It's my tooth," roared Leo.

"Come on," said Mum, "Giraffe is going to help us hang it from the magic tree, so the tooth fairy can collect it."

"But I want to keep my wobbly tooth!" cried Leo.

"You'll grow another one soon," said Mum. "And I'm sure the tooth fairy will leave you a lovely surprise when she comes to collect your tooth tonight."

That night, Leo and Mum sat by the magic tree. Leo didn't take his eyes off his tooth. Where was his surprise? What would it be?

Suddenly, a silvery, glittery light streaked across the night sky. Leo looked up in wonder. "OOOOH!" he gasped. "What was that?"

"That was the tooth fairy bringing your surprise," said Mum. "And look – your tooth has gone!"

Sure enough, in place of the tooth, a shiny star-shaped badge hung from the tree.

"This is brilliant," said Leo. "I can't *wait* for my other teeth to wobble!"

Leo's list

Things I want for my birthday
(please, Mum):

A sunny morning, a shooting star,
A thrilling daytrip (not too far),
Time to romp and wrestle and play,
A spell to make my brother go away…
I want to roar and roar and roar,
*I want a badge to say, **I'M FOUR**.*

I want my friends to come and play,
To eat jelly and crisps and stay all day,
Dozens of prizes – I'll win each one,
Otherwise it'll spoil my fun,
Lots of songs for us to sing,
*A funny hat which says **I'M KING**.*

Moochy mud and hidey-holes

Zebra looked at Leo's garden.

"What a dreadful mess!" he said.
"All those hidey-holes and little
rocks. All that water and sludgy
brown mud.

"MY garden's so neat and nice. It's
just right for a quiet snooze and a
sit in the sun."

"Grrmph," thought Leo, "my garden's all right… I'll make it the best garden ever. Just you wait and see."

And he set to work, drying out the sludgy mud, tidying up the little rocks and filling in the hidey-holes.

"What are you doing, Leo?"
asked Crocodile, walking by.

"I'm draining the water," said Leo.

"But all the best gardens have water
to splish-and-splash about in,"
said Crocodile. And he plunged into
the pond…

KERPLOSH!

"What are you doing, Leo?" asked Hippo, stopping to look.

"I'm drying out the mud," said Leo.

"But all the best gardens have sludgy mud to mess about in," said Hippo. And he mooched into the mud…

GLOOP GLOOP

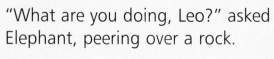

"What are you doing, Leo?" asked Elephant, peering over a rock.

"I'm tidying up the little rocks," said Leo.

"But all the best gardens have little rocks to lollop over," said Elephant, lolloping over the little rocks…

KERPLONK!

"What are you doing, Leo?" asked Baby Leopard, peeping through the gate.

"I'm filling in the hidey-holes," said Leo.

"But all the best gardens have hidey-holes," said Baby Leopard. "Please don't fill them in. You'll spoil our fun."

Leo wasn't sure what to do.

"You don't want a garden like Zebra's," said Hippo. "It's *too* tidy. It hasn't got water, or any mud, and it hasn't got little rocks to lollop over."

"And it hasn't got any hidey-holes!" cried Baby Leopard.

"Your garden's got *EVERYTHING* we need!" said Crocodile.

"They're right," thought Leo.

GLOOP! he mooched into the mud with Hippo… KERPLONK! he lolloped over the little rocks with Elephant… WHOOSH! he hid in the hidey-holes with Baby Leopard…

"I don't need a neat and tidy garden like Zebra's!" he cried. "*THIS* is the best garden ever!"

I'm me!

I'm small and spotty.

I'm tall and dotty.

I'm black and white stripey.

I'm all grey and plain.

*And **my** name is LEO and I'm a proud lion. I'm grrrmphy and grrrowly with a big furry mane.*

Well done, Leo

One day as Leo was jogging down the road he noticed a big sign that said:

THIS WAY TO OSTRICH'S GYM CLASS

"A gym class will be really easy for me," he said, chuckling. "Lions are best at everything."

Ostrich was at the front of the class fluffing her feathers.

"Everybody *stretch* as high as you can!" she called.

Leo tried very, very hard but Giraffe was the best at stretching.

"Grrmph," muttered Leo. "It's not fair."

Elephant could lift the heaviest weights with his trunk, and Hippo was absolutely brilliant at rolling over on his big fat tummy.

"Grrmph," thought Leo, "it's not fair. Maybe I'm not the best after all."

Just then everyone heard a cry, and it seemed to be coming from a long way away.

"It's Baby Leopard!" said Giraffe.
"He's stuck on top of the big rock.
Come on, we'll have to be quick."

Leo gave a loud *ROAR* to tell Baby
Leopard they were coming to
rescue him. Then he ran as fast as
the wind. All the other animals
ran behind him.

"Well done, Leo," said Elephant.
"I wish I could roar like you."

"Well done, Leo," said Hippo.
"I wish I could run like you."

"Well done, Leo," said Giraffe.
"You are the best at running and
roaring!"

"Yes, well done," said Ostrich.
"You see, Leo, everyone can find out
what they are good at if they try."

I'm coming after you!

Vultures scream
And hyenas giggle.
Elephants trumpet
And snakes wriggle.
*How does a lion say, "I'm **FOUR**!"*
*Listen, can you hear him? Lions… **ROAR**!*

Zebras run
And hippos sleep.
Giraffes stretch
And crocodiles creep.
What does a four year old lion do?
*He roars, "**I'M COMING AFTER YOU**!"*